HUMANITARIUM

by

Charles Rhodes Jamison

www.CreateSpace.com/7811571

ISBN-13: 978-0999710807
ISBN-10: 099971080X

Dedicated to my strong and cherishable Mother.

$\mathcal{A}$ dark evening brings forth a star. A night sky becomes dotted with twinkling satellites. A firefly alights on a tall blade of grass. A young boy captures the insect and places the firefly in a Mason Jar. He closes the lid. He holds up the jar and looks closely. Suddenly a bright beam encapsulates him. The boy drops the jar and ascends up a spaceship. The light vanishes, leaving the lightening bug beside a patch of grass and secured in the boy's Mason Jar. When the lad completes ascent, he has been shrunk. Simultaneously, he is contained in a jar (similar to the firefly's jar on Earth) and quickly tossed in a disorganized pile. There are countless jars surrounding the young boy in his empty capsule with other earthlings around. Some humans are frantically banging on the glass of their container. A young girl, in her transparent chamber, presses directly against the boy's jar. She sulks and holds her head downward. The disruptive means of conveyance halts. The heap of clear jars each containing a solo human moves by two bodies who apparently operate the spaceship.

The pile tumbles into a large bin. The young boy is on top of the pile. The bin tumbles on a conveyor belt. Moments later, the bundle lands on a mound of jars in a brightly lit squalid room. From the boy's perspective, the sight is disgusting. Wrappers, globs of fudge, syrup, ice cream and chips are strewn everywhere and covers half the area.

The other half has jars of modern day homo sapiens, now much smaller, held captive. A horrid looking creature enters. The grotesque beast with sharp teeth has scales, tentacles and a mouth covered in foam and slobber. The creature sinisterly glances at the new arrivals. The ghastly beast stomps toward the bunch of humans. It grabs a jar with a despondent grown woman and closely gazes at her.

It removes the lid and tosses the woman down its throat. The callous creature reaches for the boy trapped in his cylindrical prison and fiercely removes the top. The vile creature pauses upon the entrance of another being entering the galactic pet shop. The being is skinny, lime green with wide eyes. The beast hands over the young boy and the lime green entity seems to be in charge.

The seemingly more gentle alien carries the young boy through a facility of robotic arms above. The tender extraterrestrial places the boy on a desk. The robotic arms reach out to the clear and rectangular boxes. The boxes are similar to aquariums or terrariums for fish and reptiles; known to the curators as HUMANITARIUMS. The neon E.T. holds the jar and slowly releases the boy in his transparent box. His empty box consists of four clear tall walls. The same alien hand which housed him places a saucer of water in his box. The alien removes its arm and closes the top. This roof of thin metal resembles a screen.

The alien bends closer to the boy's humanitarium and looks directly at the boy. The boy goggles at eyes which stretch the entire width of his front wall. He sits with legs and arms folded thus never breaking his stare with the alien. A small stir occurs. The alien turns around and communicates with three humanoid buyers. Two customers are tall and one is little. The little one, with a vigorous smile, has pigtails. Evidently the tall figures are the parents of the exuberant girl who points to the young boy behind the desk. The lime green attendant shakes its head, implying "No."

The attendant leads the colorful family down an aisle. The boy beholds the scene, which wrings his heart. Thousands of humans are held hostage and confined in humanitariums. Horrified, he observes the diminutive pigtails pointing decisively to a tank. The neon attendant nods, presses a button and retrieves a jar. The galactic customers process their transaction. The commodity is quite obvious. The family of three purchase a frantic, crying and screaming earthling.

As the human disappears, the boy witnesses the childish customer holding the jar nigh to her eye. Lettuce and potatoes are thrown in the boy's tank and fortunately the vegetables are the right size. Whirling above rapidly, the machines feed all the eye can see. The lights, computers and machines turn off. Silence spreads throughout the vast facility. Before the boy can digest what occurred to him the previous hour, he hears a bang followed by a loud boom.

The repetitive sound gradually pervades the area. Silence falls for a moment, then the rhapsodic vibration continues. The boy can only imagine the source of the sound. He trembles in terror and sweats from dread. He curbs his fright when he picks up a humanly cadence. The boy smiles once singing begins and then joins with a tapping foot. The song becomes louder which originated from the ulterior perimeter. He feels the symphony coming from his surrounding tank mates.

In the darkness he can't determine more than a resonating chorus of songs combined with drums. The young boy can't resist the urge to stand up and move his feet to the beat. He sways and plays along for hours until he succumbs to exhaustion. He lies flat on his back without a pillow or sack. The young boy, Jack, sleeps soundly as a bat.

Jack awakens to the same green eyes peering through his tank and a soft tap on the glass. The lights turn on and rows of metal arms trolley back and forth. The arms are dispensing corn, tomatoes, green leaves and sprays the humanitariums with water. Despite his captivity and new stature, Jack examines his only choice of subsistence. He smells the scent of fresh vegetables. Jack sits and eats. He peeks at his enormous caretaker communicating with other kindred beings. Every exchange has the same result. A human is desired to be purchased. The humanoids exit with their newly acquired earthling. Humans respond differently to their unknown fate.

Jack laughs at a portly gentleman during a transaction. Jack thinks the man can pass out any second. The confined man, with his thick beard, belts out Italian opera notes. Dangling from his beard are crumbs of food. When he catches his breath, the singer swills.

A spectacle to behold, Jack swears he sees a roman gladiator in a jar on a nearby shelf. Next to the gladiator: a pirate, pharaoh, warrior and monk. He becomes distracted when noticing a woman leaping side to side tightly in a corner. She continues the activity for hours in her tank with other humans. The tank mates watch her burst of energy and flexibility. She makes her way to the top. Twenty yards away from Jack, the intrepid woman grabs the screen and wails aloud a boisterous moan propelled by melancholy. She doesn't call out a name or word. The long note from her sends goosebumps spreading on Jack's body.

More water is placed in Jack's wooden bowl from the daunting hand. This is the only item accompanying Jack. His heart beats like a rabbit as he absorbs the scale of the neon giant. When the worker becomes distracted from a duty outside the desk, Jack imbibes the conduct of various human behavior. Jack notices the woman who made the indelible sound now clouts the top of the screen lid. The typically dormant crowd below her cheers upwards. Their uproar gives the acrobatic damsel the strength to tear the rim with her bare hands. An acclamation ejaculates inside one of the many tanks.

The event and attention turns into madness when the brave heroine forces her torso through the tight lid. Cheering and chanting erupts as she squeezes her legs to escape. Jack, can't resist or ignore his urge to participate in the cheer. Jack understands the fuss. The fervor is for the dame who made her dwelling lame; for without any luck, she used her internal pluck. She looks below at a throng gathering beneath to cop a better view of her. The creature returns to its desk. The free woman furtively sidles backwards and tucks behind a rock. Next to the rock are smaller pebbles and boulders. Tiny trees, logs and sticks are above her on a shelf. Lights cease as machines become still. Darkness begins.

Tonight, there is no sound or movement similar to last night. The eerie silence disappoints Jack. He plops down on the smooth floor hoping a song breaks out and thinking of the courageous soul who escaped. He can't sleep. Jack reclines on his back. He closes his eyes and envisions stars. He focuses to capture a twinkle; his hope fades as their is no astral spectacle to behold. Only on Earth do objects dazzle a night sky... so Jack begins to cry.

Bionic movement stirs and the store illuminates to start a new day. The same giant creature glides by the counter and begins work. From Jack's perspective, there are no glass windows. The unjustly overbearing fluorescent lights are controlled by a timer. Jack painfully squints around; in hopes for natural light, but artificial glow has too much to show. Although the room is a pleasant temperature, he wants to escape the fluorescent radiance. Jack eases up to the routine arm at work replacing the heap of rotting food and stands firmly under the worker's hand being raised. He is happy for a moment and stares at the wrinkled hand. The limb finishes a clean sweep. Jack turns his hands over to study his own palms.

An unearthly group approaches the vicinity of Jack and points curiously. Language is inaudible; however, a hum can be detected. The clerk stretches near Jack to retrieve an unfortunate human. The worker reaches for the jar containing an unfamiliar woman. This person stands akimbo, sporting a fancy cap adorned with a feather. Jack throws himself against the thick acrylic. He presses his chest against the wall, bending his neck to his shoulder. He pops his eyes at the woman. She solemnly displays her cheek and lifts her countenance, followed by a sincere curtsy. Subsequently, she is taken away.

Jack is visibly emotional. He contemplates over the daredevil freely skulking on the nearby shelf. Jack, darting his eyes left to right, scans up and down. He locates the woman.

She is alive, well and standing still at the base of an ornamental tree. The relatively large tree is void of fruit and leaves. Jack vigorously waves to capture her attention, but she disappears. The tank she was standing on creates a frenzy. The humans are pushing and shoving each other. Jack is interested and treads along one side of his wall. He acquires a better angle to spy on the spectacle. A man shouts over the disorderly conduct. A few hurl themselves at the man's side. He calmly ushers the individuals respectfully to retain a new position.

One by one, a bedlam waxes a lineup consisting of rows. Jack witnesses a prior gaggle become a well structured pyramid. A humanly bundle coalesced by the voice box of a spirit. The pack clings together and extends vertically. The soulful leader climbs slowly to the top, via a human ladder. He escapes through a hole previously created overnight by the liberated acrobat above. Jack jumps excitedly. The leader fades away in the distance on the shelf.

Jack cannot see the two humans on the adjacent shelves, but objects in the area shake and fall. A branch from a tree snaps. A stone thrown to a boulder splits asunder. Jack's attention diverts to a corner below the happening shelf. A maverick dispassionately buffets his cell. Jack can perceive the red hair brute gripping two potatoes with clinched fists and bleeding knuckles. Although the day passes; the entertainment does not.

Rumbling pervades during Jack's third night. Hollering jolts him intermittently, still he manages to rest. Again, avian twitter doesn't awake Jack in the morning. Instead, he embraces the same stare down versus the large creature secured within his glassy humanitarium.

Jack observes the first arriving customers for the day. Their manner is somewhat   dignified. The pair of customers walk to the main counter. They distract the attendant and Jack paces in his daily empiricism. The boxer across the way, actuates his usual combat until the structure cracks around him. Because of this, he is vibrantly wrought up and increases his speed. The boxer's back wall collapses. Subsequently, he too falls to the ground of his slammer.

Weird entertainment deflects Jack's hunger. Rather than eating, Jack craves for the burly boxer to stand and march to freedom. There is no movement from the pug. The previous two escapees run to and fro. The man carries a spear and the woman holds a stony blade. Jack gains their heed pointing calmly beneath their feet. The wild man and woman creep along together.

The pair of alien customers amble behind the head clerk and consider their purchase. The person sits Indian-style and retained in a jar. The human has a meek attitude of accepting her unknowable fate. Jack does not wish to be purchased.

Business is slow, so the fostering figure removes Jack's lid and prostrates its hand on Jack's floor, palm up. Jack examines before leaping playfully on the open limb. He obtains a better view given his preferential treatment. Jack searches for the armed beatniks. His last vision of the duo left him breathless. During the process of unobstructed vision, the worker gives Jack a different snack. He is offered fruit and Jack gladly accepts. The nectarine has juicy sweetness. Jack's brain is stimulated from the citric sugar galvanizing a grin. This pleases the worker.

Jack notices the formerly passed out boxer no longer lays motionless. Whether he sallied forth, Jack does not know.

He silently prays thus be the rogue's case. Hours pass and the computers subside.

Jack returns to his cell and his friendly foe departs for the evening. The regular machines cease and the lights quickly vanish. No sound for hours. Jack reminisces about the orchestra created by frogs and crickets at night back home. He yearns for the sun to collimate at dawn while birds chirp and his canine rolls in the dirt. He pines for life on Earth.

As Jack awakes the next day, the handy brawler emerges from fluttering luminance and climbs a counter. The other male running amok, sprints nearby and heads in the same locale. A tank surrounded by slabs of rock gives them an inclination to go higher. The man showcased by his held torch travels one direction. The bare knuckle hitter trots aggressively up a rocky ramp on the other side. The metallic computers and synthetic limbs give rise to a novel day.

The neon employee arrives rattled and aware the store is amiss. The clerk scans quickly and targets the woman. She swiftly changes her direction and heads toward the men. All three run upward unaware they will soon meet on a higher plane. The three rascals are driven by fear of losing liberty. They focus on what's behind them. When they almost collide, the scalawags face off. They immediately furrow their brows, but then rapidly bow. Aligning back to back, the boxer bobs his rocking shoulders that power his fists. The daring lass cocks her dagger. The dude pounds the base of his spear on the floor which adjoins a sonic roar.

The worker covers the trio with a jar, slides paper underneath and carries them to its desk. It places the three that broke out in the container along with Jack. The man and woman stand in opposite corners.

Jack and the boxer are loitering silently on the other side. The woman studies her new obstacle. The man in the corner kicks and feels out his new tank. A minute passes and the Irish, weathered and freckled boxer speaks,

"Well, that was an interesting night. How do you do, lad, Arthur O' Shannon."
Jack, a scrawny teen with short dirty hair, replies,
"Jack Spencer."
"Well, Jack Spencer, I presume you have been shanghaied by the same skunks that took me. Perhaps in your case at a different time, given your unusual attire."

Jack looks down at his ensemble about to speak; he pauses at the appearance of the attendant. The attendant places dirt on the floor of their humanitarium, adding sticks, logs, vegetables and water dish. The man and woman in opposite corners snap out of their deep thought as they gravitate toward the center. The man picks up a small amount of dirt, he smells and tastes the dirt. The woman sits and eats. Her back is to the group. Jack and Arthur sit on stumps.

A bell chimes and a small creature skips toward the counter carrying a jar with a familiar woman sporting a large hat with a feather. Jack witnesses the body language. The customer wants to exchange its purchase for another human. The attendant makes the exchange.

The customer leaves and attendant places returned woman in the humanitarium with the others. The woman removes her hat, curtsies and says,

"Greetings to whom are present." Arthur says,
"Hello, fine lady."
Jack speaks in the wake of Arthur's verbal announcement,

"Yes, hello. Hello!"

Arthur whispers to Jack,
"Grab this favorite form of heroine a seat."
Jack hastily grabs a stump, moving quickly, he stumbles and
stubs his toe. He gesticulates the offer of a seat; places the
stump between Jack and Arthur and says,
"Please."
Arthur stands up, places one hand over his heart and one behind
his back as Jack observes. She sits down and says,
"Gentlemen", removes her hat, crosses her legs and looks
straight ahead with no expression. The tall woman has long,
voluminous hair and a dark olive complexion.

Arthur, still standing,
"Arthur O'Shannon from the land of Ire, how do you do
madam?"
"María Castillo De La Cruz of Hispaniola."

Arthur looks at Jack and tacitly inspires him to declare himself.

"Jack Spencer, from Delaware."
Arthur and Maria say to themselves dubiously,
"Delaware?"

Arthur looks at Jack.
"Jack Spencer, help me split these logs, soon we shall have a
fire."
Jack begins to break down logs and develops a center. Arthur
places two additional stumps to complete a circle.

The humanitarium trembles as the attendant approaches and opens the lid to place twigs, palm leaves and a bowl of water opposite the water and food dishes. Maria takes interest in the water bowl, stands up and slowly tests the water while making a clothesline using her belt and two sticks. She hangs her hat on a stick. She slowly disrobes, washes each article of clothing and hangs those to dry on the line. As she covers herself with fabric, she wades in the water to bathe.

Jack and Arthur are working on the fire pit. Arthur admonishing quietly tells Jack,
"A lady will stop if you gawk; eyes at the fire, Mr. Jack Spencer. Keep your thoughts as clean as she does her body."

Arthur, mistakenly glances at Maria. He catches his slip up and returns to gazing at the fire. Jack titters as the strong, bald, dark and lean man approaches and spins his spear 360 degrees. He forces the spire into the dirt; sits on the ground in front of a stump, appreciates the fire and says,

"Aman, Africa."

The other woman sports a dagger, long hair and pony tail tied atop. She stands up, eating a potato, bows to the group and brings Aman a potato as she sits on a stump.
Jack blurts,
"I am itching for it. Ma'am, if you can, please indulge us. What may we call you and where are you from?"

"Yoshi Kumiko, Japan."

Maria approaches last remaining stump, brings a stick, places hat on stick, sits on the stump, gracefully crossing her legs looking at the group.

"Aman, Yoshi, a true pleasure of making your acquaintance has taken place. I am, María Castillo De La Cruz, of Hispaniola."

Yoshi stands up, holding a trencher; Jack accepts food. Arthur says,

"Ms. Yoshi you are good with that blade."

Yoshi nods and Maria picks up her head,
"Perhaps 'tis best for you to fabricate a sword for me to vest."

Yoshi bows,
"Most certainly."
After passing the food around, she places the trencher in front of Aman and takes a seat next to him. Aman bites into a tomato and laughs. Yoshi laughs while patting Aman on the back. Aman nods to Yoshi. With Yoshi's hand on Aman's shoulder she announces, "Our trencherman!"

"What is it?" says Arthur to Aman.
"A very good batch. As much as I miss our planet, my soil was not rich. I could not grow vegetables like this."
Arthur replies,
"I understand, then again I don't. From where I hail, plants and herbs grow as far as the eye can see."

Jack glances at Arthur and Aman,
"My father grows corn. I help my mother with the shucking. I never liked it before until now. I sort of miss it, I wonder if she is doing that now or if she is worried about me and not shucking the corn my pa grows."

Jack gets choked up and Arthur pats Jack on the back.
"Chin up, lad. One day soon you will see your family again. I too miss my dear."

Jack asks Arthur,

"You have reindeer? What do they eat?" "No, No good lad, I mean my darling. The better half of me in a female form, my sweetheart... my corn shucker." Arthur continues,

"How about you madam Castillo, what back on Earth do you miss most?"
"I miss the spray off my bow. Oceanic mist driven by spindrift, catching last rays from the setting sun; casting a rainbow by the only one."
Aman says,
"I too miss water and Ra."

Yoshi stands, stokes the fire,
"I have a young boy to watch turn into a man. A boy who needs his mother. By God, I will get back to him."

Arthur looks at Yoshi.
"Look around, I don't think God exists."

Yoshi responds,
"I intend on finding out. If Jehovah be true, then the almighty will help us reunite with the ones we knew."
Yoshi points to a corner of the humanitarium.
"I am not impressed by the scale of what contains us. I am impressed by the characters I now reside beside. With your help and the avail of Maria's great Redeemer, we shall all see home and the ones we love again."
Maria says affirmatively, "Hear...Here."

The hand opens the lid and as smoke clears, the fire pit is smothered. All five freeze simultaneously. Rocks are dispersed by caretaker's appendage. Burning coal scatters and becomes cool. Aman, not so cool. He burns more intensely than the fire which brought them all warmth and comfort. If Aman were at home in Ethiopia, he would work his arms, legs and back to the bone in order to provide for the family he cares for so much. When his day came to a close in Ethiopia and duties along with children were still, he put together a fire almost every night. He sat outside under the stars in perfect contentment, feeling the warmth of the blaze as if a simple man from Ethiopia created a sun at night.

Aman's rage reaches boiling point. He managed to build a fire after years of other worldly captivity; only to have it snuffed out the very moment he was beginning to smile. And so it goes, he rears back his primitive prick and shoves the tip with a twist of his wrist on the alien's finger tip…yea. He watches the alien flinch, then violently flicks Aman against the side of the hominid terrarium.

The coexisting company, still frozen, look at Aman on the floor. He rises slowly with the help of his staff and gently smiles.

Today is a busy day in the galactic pet shop filled with an assortment of humans. The caretaker behind the desk has a curious customer. The other shoppers had others with them. This alien customer, first to walk in alone, appears softer. The pitch resonates from the walls of the humanitarium which comes from the creature nearby. Usually this sound is low and makes the humans fearful. Even one such as Aman.

The curious little creature (attributing a dulcet voice) is about four feet tall and advances to the counter. Jack creeps to the glass and looks directly at the new guest. Suddenly with a locked stare on Jack, the small alien points at him. The caretaker turns swiftly to open the lid and reaches in. Jack springs into action to evade. He rolls one way, flips another while the creature is amused, watching Jack dodge, duck and dive. Eventually Jack loses steam and grows jaded.

The hand grasps Jack tightly and throws him in a small clear box for closer inspection. Jack stands tall. He remembers Maria's heroic demeanor when he first laid eyes on her. He picks up his chin in tribute to the memory of such a fine woman. With that inner strength he looks over at his companions in the larger structure.

Arthur O'Shannon salutes Jack. Aman raises his spear. Yoshi holds a high fist in the air next to Maria who gazes at Jack with a stolid tear, standing strong as always. Jack barely knew the four he spent one day and night with, but boy did his heart ache as he knew deep down, he would never see their faces again. He will miss Arthur's exemplary disposition of masculinity along with Arthur's enchanting words of wisdom. Jack will most certainly remember Yoshi's face. She never smiled or laughed, yet her presence brought Jack much warmth. Yoshi loves her children and her life at home; without such, Miss Yoshi would wilt. No doubt Jack will never forget Aman. The light reflects off Aman in a way unlike the others. A moment went by last night (at peak of the fire) when Jack looked solemnly at everyone circling around the pit and saw an even more intense glow emanating from Aman. Without any question, Jack will miss the figure of Maria the most.

In a split second when Jack does not look at the group, the crew goes out of sight. This happens so quickly. Jack fills himself with worry and becomes sick. He looks around at the empty surrounding. Jack is on a shelf in a small clear cube. Two eyes gradually rise. Green pupils with white eyes stare intently at

Jack. Both hands are placed on the glass. The green eyes have hands. Jack prays silently those hands will be benevolent.

Food rains down. A tomato to the left, corn to the right. Jack observes the main caretaker behind the counter as he approaches and sprays the walls of Jack's tiny enclosure. The walls are dripping wet. The clear cube moves and then goes dark. The movement makes Jack think he is in a pocket. Truth be told, Jack wishes he is in the pocket of the new creature. The eyes being different from the rest of the customers that visit the shop. All the other visitors he considered monstrous in appearance. Instead of red eyes, this creature has green. In place of a hideous mouth with vicious teeth, this one choosing Jack has a puny mouth and no visible teeth. Just gums and a tongue.

During the bumpy ride, Jack tumbles from side to side. He eventually covers his head with his hands until finally the cube stops. Slowly removing his fixed arms around his precious skull, Jack relaxes his tired muscles. Never had he flexed his abdomen for so long in order to absorb an unpredictable jerk. He thinks if only he had been placed in the pocket without the case; this probably would have made for a fun trip. Perhaps able to peek out and not be trapped in a tight box.

Jack's breathing changes to a slower pace. Confusion sets in. Jack can't manage to draw a deep breath. He is choking and can't breathe. He can not breathe. All the air he inhales has already been exhaled. He then collapses.

The cover is removed and light beams in with a gust of fresh air just in time to bring Jack back to life. Relieved, Jack stands up to look around the room. Strangely, the room appears as his, in a way. The other worldly being has: knick knacks, pictures, trophies, memorabilia, clothes and a skateboard. Trippy.

The clear cube containing Jack turns on its side to be placed in a larger humanitarium with walls of clear glass and a high ceiling. Jack notices a screen lid at the top. After all he has been through, missing his family is not on his mind. He is hungry and can't stand the sight of what lays at his feet. Corn and tomatoes are great, but not everyday for God's sake. Nothing in Jack's space but rotten tomatoes along with foul smelling corn. He remembers the smell of his mother's banana pancakes wafting in the air.

Jack longs for meat, bread and soup; although tasty and plentiful as his ideal meal might be, 'tis best served with the ones he loves.

The lights shut off while the new caretaker turns in for the night. No blanket or pillow. Back at the shop Aman gave Jack a log to rest his head and Maria had an extra piece of fabric for his cold feet. Here, now, nothing other than decomposing food and miserable Jack. Jack begins to cry again. This time he can't bear never seeing his friends and family and so an added groan creates a wailing sound. The scream wakes the sleeping alien. With the lights back on, the angry alien slaps the humanitarium. Jack goes silent along with his hopes.

Somehow Jack catches some shut eye and awakes to a lively scene. Obviously this new creature is part of a family. A novel one pops its head in. The head peeks quickly at the door and vanishes. It reappears and slowly moves to a shelf near Jack's humanitarium. Scary eyes stare at Jack. The horrifying face smiles, exposing sharp teeth. Returning from the hallway, the friendly form drops fresh tomatoes inside with Jack after waving off ominous stranger. The green eyes look at Jack for a moment. Jack picks up one and hurls a tomato.

The tomato splatters along his front wall. The alien's face recoils in surprise. Some satisfaction runs through Jack and he chucks another until no tomatoes are at his feet. A paste covers the front wall of Jack's humanitarium. Finally some privacy, he thinks.

The creature leaves confused while Jack sulks throughout the day leaving him alone and thirsty. His new owner returns and opens the lid. Jack can hardly open his eyes. The hand gently nudges Jack, testing for life. After the third attempt, the hand is slapped. A dish of water is set in the corner with a few rocks. Walls are wiped clean and floor cleared by owner's appendage. Immediately Jack approaches the water dish and splashes his face. Refreshment hits him and brings about a grin. Jack hops in the bowl of mother nature's most divine creation.

The water is fine. He splashes for awhile, getting a kick out of the sight and sound. He then thinks where is some meat and cheese or bread topped with seeds? His cravings drive him nuts. Jack imagines a feast in front of his water dish.

Nothing except plain glass occupies his cell until Jack picks up a scent. He lifts his nose and sniffs repeatedly. The top is removed and a food dish is placed in another corner. Oh don't let it be tomatoes and corn! Something salty please, perhaps a sweet treat or maybe a piece of delicious meat. As he guesses what could be, Jack swirls in his bowl. He notices those big green eyes staring diligently. He can't help but feel some slight appreciation. After all the water is warm and clean. Possibly whatever is in his food dish is tasty. A closer look and Jack knows the smell of bread. He grabs a roll with each hand. He returns to the water dish with a piece of sourdough in each palm. Jack jumps in making a splash. The alien's hand reaches down and wipes the floor dry. Topping off Jack's day, a bundle of fresh hay is laid in order to cushion his stay. Sure doesn't beat life at home on Earth, but good enough for now.

Artificial radiance dims and the extraterrestrial goes to sleep. Making do with his current situation at night, Jack nestles to sleep. When the room's door opens slightly, a dark figure encroaches the humanitarium. A bright light flashes on Jack. Blinded by the light, Jack squirms for a decent glance at the source. Spotlight ceases and shines again. The door closes and Jack sleeps for the night.

Day begins and Jack is slow to rise for the morning routine. Jack's keeper walks out. How did Jack spend his day? How would you or anyone? Once fed he wants out and does what Arthur O'Shannon did for freedom. He tries to pound his way out with his own fists. Jack tries and can't even make a dent. He picks up a rock and smashes it against the side with no crack inflicted. Jack looks up and around. He turns over his water dish and drags the bread bowl. He builds a tower. When he reaches the top, he discovers the metal wire is too tough. He climbs down, tucks himself in; then he plots improvements for an escape during tomorrow's endeavors. A smoldering rock will do the trick. How can he grab hold of a hot rock and climb? This single thought gave way to a good night's rest; until the annoying flicker of the spotlight. The light during the day, brought on by the young keeper, is welcome but not during the night. An entity of some kind comes in and flashes light. Sure this is a harmless act, but oh so irksome.

Next day, the hand pauses to place the palm upward. The hand inches closer to Jack. Jack steps back. With a closer look, the hand has prints and lines similar to a human.

Jack thinks the cup of the palm seems cozy. So why not? It really can't get much worse and here is a way out. Jack is brought to eye level on the keeper's hand. The two no longer look at each other, but through one another. The sweet creature smiles when Jack gestures up yours!

Large books are stacked in front of the humanitarium. Each book is one hundred times larger than Jack, but regular size to the alien. Opening a book, the alien studies both pages and Jack's humanitarium until a knock on Jack's door. A rolling robot enters the room holding a large bag and exits.

The keeper removes each item one by one. Jack watches from his enclosure and notices every object. A bag of something brown comes from above. Jacks moves aside to make room for dirt. A thick layer of earthy dirt is at Jack's feet instead of the glass floor. The eyes lower on forearms and absorbs Jack's body language. Squeezing his toes in the dirt for the first time, Jack screams loudly at the peering keeper,
"Hey, what about my hay?"

The alien replaces the water dish and food bowl. This time potatoes are substituted for bread. Jack's stomach grumbles for steak, chicken, fish, pork or stork, anything but the same staple. A craving for fruit and all its variety spurs Jack to throw potatoes at surrounding walls. He uses his hand to scrape off the residue and shoves mashed potatoes in his mouth. The alien watches in amazement and smiles once again.

A window in Jack's room suggests the planet has a day to night cycle. The room shines red from the outdoors. Even though Jack is hungry, he has a strong desire to gaze out the window. A pile of logs is added to Jack's tank. Frustrated, Jack breaks a log against a side wall. When day ends, Jack sees the same flashing light in the middle of the night.

The next morning, the alien awakes quickly. Darting his green eyes to Jack's container, the keeper notices Jack is gone. The young creature runs to the glass box on the shelf. He does not see Jack. The keeper hastily digs in the dirt. He flips over dishes and makes a mess. Calmly, the alien moves its head to survey the room. Jack, with eyes wide open, is at the window. While the alien advances to the window, Jack can't keep his eyes away from the view outside. The planet is red and rocky. Sand covers the landscape for miles.

At the window sill, the large alien and small human look at one another kindly. The one who purchased Jack begins tidying the disheveled humanitarium. It levels the surface and adjusts the dishes.

Jack's holder displays its palm so he can take Jack back. Jack gives him a shaking fist and moves away from the palm. Upon nudging, Jack concedes and returns to his humanitarium.

A rock with a sharp edge helped him escape. He cut the wires after climbing to the top. When Jack tore away at the wires, he stashed a few in his pocket. He fastens three wires tightly around the split log and puts together a makeshift guitar. He has a sip of water and begins to sing as the alien keeper leans in curiously.

"Hey there nice face, take me back to my native place where fruit grows and animals play, for here I don't want to stay."

The music strikes a chord in the alien. The keeper runs out and brings company to Jack's room. An older biological being enters with known caretaker. This figure carries a flashlight strapped around its waist. It walks with a stick made of wood. Jack's eyes latch on the walking stick. The two imposing occupants walk up to Jack's humanitarium. The young one taps on the glass. Jack drops his instrument, moves to front wall and begins to breathe out creating a patch of condensation. Jack, using his finger, writes on the moisture. The word Earth is spelled out. Jack steps back, picks up his instrument and starts singing the same song. The two aliens of same skin and eyes, possessing kindred behavior, smile at Jack in amusement. The pair leave, lights dim and Jack pouts all night.

Next morning, something is wrong with Jack. He sits and does not eat. Minutes pass and keeper exits the room. Moments later, the keeper returns with the alien of older characteristics. The flash light strapped around the elder's waist, shines on Jack. Jack blocks the light with his forearms. Staggering to the front wall, Jacks exhales heavily on the glass wall. He spells out Earth again and sits somberly. The elder being leans in. A talisman hanging on a chain around the alien's neck bangs up against a shelf near Jack's humanitarium. Jack notices the charm ornamenting the creature is a human skeleton.

The following day, Jack refuses to eat. The young keeper looks intently at Jack. Appearing frail and unrecognizable, Jack stares upward. His eyes filled and cheeks covered with tears. He lets out a bone chilling moan which causes the alien onlooker to recoil.

Jack wails for hours on end. When night arrives, the spotlight appears. A giant, wrinkled, green and open hand is offered inside the humanitarium. Dazed and confused, Jack flounders onto the palm. He is placed in a cozy pocket. Catching a glance of the walking stick, Jack knows he is on the waist of the elder accompanying the young keeper. A loud rumble shakes Jack to the core. The mechanical vibration stops after an hour. Jack sleeps from infirmity. A hand cups Jack's small body.

His limbs hang off the sides of the young alien's hand. Jack opens his eyes and slowly touches the nose of the innocent extraterrestrial. The elder places his hand underneath the cupped palm and he too looks fondly at Jack. The two giant liberators place Jack on the same tube from the beginning of Jack's journey. Pressing a button beside the tubular platform, Jack shoots downward onto earthy grass. He is back to his former size. A mason jar, at his feet, contains a lightning bug. He bends down to open the jar. The bug escapes and flashes alongside his benevolent ride in the night sky, fading by distance -

Jack says,

"Goodbye."

www.ingramcontent.com/pod-product-compliance
Lightning Source LLC
Chambersburg PA
CBHW071629140626
46555CB00021B/1933